The Yellow River

The Yellow River

Kim Dramer

Franklin Watts
A Division of Grolier Publishing
New York • Hong Kong • Sydney
Danbury, Connecticut

For my father

Note to readers: Definitions for words in **bold** can be found in the Glossary at the back of this book.

Photographs ©: Art Resource, NY: 26, 42 (Werner Forman Archive/Private Collection); Asia Access/Naomi Duguid: 28, 29; China Span/Keren Su: 5 right, 14, 38; China Stock: 27, 46 (Dennis Cox), 16 (Liu Liqun), 18 (Wang Lu), 51 left, 9, 20, 21 (Yang Xiuyun); Christie's Images: 19; Corbis-Bettmann: 40 (Jack Fields), 49 (Julia Waterlow, Eye Ubiquitous); Liaison Agency, Inc.: 51 (Xinhua/Chine Nouvel), 35 (Francois Perri/GLMR); Mountain Light/Galen Rowell: 12; Network Aspen/Jeffrey Aaronson: 37; Panos Pictures: 48 (Alain le Garsme), 10, 11 (Chris Stowers); Photo Researchers/Lowell Georgia: cover; Stone/Jerry Alexander: 25; Superstock, Inc.: 34; Wolfgang Kaehler: 2, 22, 30, 33.

Calligraphy courtesy of the John S. T. Wang.
Map by Bob Italiano.

The photograph on the cover shows a boat on the Yellow River in Jinan. The photograph opposite the title page shows the Yellow River near Lanzhou.

> Visit Franklin Watts on the Internet at:
> http://publishing.grolier.com

Library of Congress Cataloging-in-Publication Data

Dramer, Kim.
　The Yellow River / by Kim Dramer
　　　p. cm.— (Watts library)
　Includes bibliographical references and index.
　ISBN 0-531-11855-X (lib. bdg.)　　0-531-13983-2 (pbk.)
　1. China—Civilization—Juvenile literature. 2. Yellow River (China)—Juvenile literature. [1. China—Civilization. 2. Yellow River (China)] I. Title. II. Series.
DS721 .D76　2001
951'.1—dc21

00-039925

© 2001 Franklin Watts, A Division of Grolier Publishing
All rights reserved. Published simultaneously in Canada.
Printed in the United States of America.
1 2 3 4 5 6 7 8 9 10 R 10 09 08 07 06 05 04 03 02 01

Contents

Chapter One
China's Sorrow 7

Chapter Two
Cradle of Civilization 13

Chapter Three
Birth of an Empire 23

Chapter Four
Sacred Sites 31

Chapter Five
In Art and Words 39

Chapter Six
Canals of the Yellow 47

52 **Timeline**

53 **Glossary**

55 **To Find Out More**

59 **A Note on Sources**

61 **Index**

Chapter One

China's Sorrow

China's Yellow River, or *Huang he*, is named for the yellow, sandy silt it carries in its water. This silt, called **loess**, is almost as fine as flour. Over thousands of years, the northwestern wind blowing from the Gobi Desert has deposited hundreds of feet of loess over northern China. As the Yellow River flows through China, it sweeps away the fine, yellow silt and carries it downriver.

The **source** of the Yellow River is in the Qinghai Province on the Tibetan

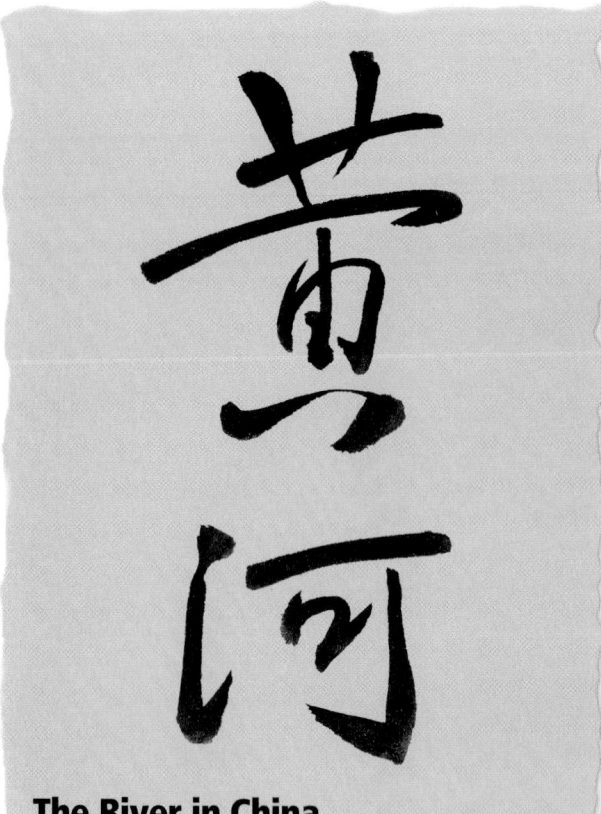

The River in China

The Chinese call the Yellow River the *Huang he*. The Chinese calligraphy for the name *Huang he* is shown above. The character below, *he*, which means "river," contains the water symbol—three drops of water joined together.

Plateau. This area is often called the "Roof of the World" because of its high altitude, the height of a place above sea level. In spring and summer, the melting snows here combine with rain and cause the waters of the Yellow River to swell. The muddy waters of the river sweep across China toward its **mouth** in the Bohai Sea.

Each year, the waters of the Yellow River carry 1.5 billion tons of silt to the Bohai Sea. The silt can make up as much as 46 percent of the water's content. Yet only about one-third of the silt carried by the Yellow River reaches the Bohai Sea. The rest sinks to the bottom of the Yellow River. These huge deposits of silt cause the riverbed to rise and change its course. As a result, the level of the Yellow's water is unstable and the river is likely to flood.

Over the centuries, flooding has caused much suffering to those living along the banks of the Yellow River. Millions of people have drowned, towns have been destroyed, and crops have been ruined. For these reasons, the river is sometimes called "China's Sorrow."

Throughout history, the Chinese have tried to tame the Yellow River. They have built a series of **dikes** to keep back

These dikes help control the waters of the Yellow River near Kaifeng.

the rising waters. In many places, the dikes have been built so high that the Yellow River actually flows from 15 to 30 feet (5 to 9 meters) above the level of surrounding land.

A man carries water from the Yellow River for farm irrigation.

However, the Yellow River also brings benefits to the Chinese. Its waters are used to irrigate the parched lands of the northern plains, allowing farmers to grow millet and

wheat. As one Chinese saying points out: "The Yellow River brings a hundred sorrows, but there is prosperity on its bend."

The Yellow River flows entirely within the borders of China, and many different aspects of Chinese life are seen along its banks. The nomads of highland China bring their flocks to drink its waters and the hard-working farmers of the northern plains use its waters to irrigate their fields. There are traditional farmers as well as farming communes organized by the government. Small villages line the river, as do large cities. Everywhere along its banks the Yellow regulates the rhythm of life for those who live by its ebb and flow.

The River at a Glance

The Yellow is 3,395 miles (5,464 kilometers) long, making it just a little shorter than the Mississippi River. It is China's second-longest river after the Yangzi and the fifth-longest river in the world.

A lone traveler walks along one of the many lakes on the Tibetan Plateau.

Chapter Two
Cradle of Civilization

The Tibetan Plateau is the highest plateau in the world and is the source for the major rivers of Asia. In the northeastern part of the plateau where the Yellow River rises, the cold, wet climate has combined with frozen soil to form a vast area of marshes and lakes. In the glittering moonlight, these marshes and lakes look like an enormous sea of stars. The Chinese call this area *Xingsuhai*, which means "the sea where the stars reside."

Traveling on Rough Waters

The upper reaches of the Yellow are known for their rushing waters—waters so fierce that the Chinese could not span the river with bridges. Instead, the Chinese in the highland area use rafts made from sheepskin sacks filled with air to travel the river.

As it cuts across the Tibetan Plateau, the Yellow flows to the southeast past Qinghai Lake—the "Dark Blue Sea." Here, the churning waters of the river match the rugged land around it. Unable to span the rough waters with bridges, the Chinese see the Yellow as a barrier to setting up communities in the area.

However, the need to control the rushing waters of the Yellow River is often used to explain the rise of Chinese civilization. In order for their civilization to flourish, the early Chinese needed to build bridges across the Yellow River for travel and communication. People had to learn how to restrain the Yellow's waters and prevent flooding. In order to feed a large community, people had to develop larger farms and grow more food. They needed water for their crops. To accomplish these goals, many people had to work together guided by a few leaders. Here, believe some scholars, are the origins of China's imperial dynasties.

Early People of the Yellow

Archaeologists have uncovered the beginnings of Chinese civilization in the Wei River Basin where the Yellow and its major **tributary**—the Wei River—meet. In this area, the ancient Chinese changed from being a roving society that hunted for and gathered food to a settled community that grew crops. And this important cultural change relied upon the waters of the Yellow River.

Archaeological sites in this area of China are always found close to the water, some dating back to the Stone Age—a time when people used tools made from polished stones. The abundance of water from Yellow and its tributaries enabled people to grow enough crops to feed a large population. Scientists have found pollen from wheat and millet at many of these archaeological sites.

In 1954, Chinese archaeologists discovered a large Stone Age community at **Banpo** where people lived from about 4800 B.C. to 4300 B.C. A ditch surrounding Banpo village protected the residents who raised millet, used stone axes, and kept dogs and pigs. Fish were caught from the nearby tributary of the Yellow River using hooks made from bones.

Artifacts found at Banpo show the importance of the Yellow River to the early Chinese. The designs and shapes of pottery found at Banpo indicate that people's lives revolved around the waters of the Yellow. They decorated many pieces of pottery with drawings of fish and made **amphorae**, or water jugs. People used the jugs to carry drinking water and water

This bowl illustrates one of the fish designs that are popular in Banpo.

Culture Heroes

Chinese myths tell stories of **culture heroes**, legendary figures who were said to have discovered fire and invented farming, hunting, and fishing. One of these mythical heroes, Yu, became known for taming the rivers of China. Yu created channels and dredged the rivers to change the flow of the Yellow and hundreds of other rivers to stop them from flooding. After completing this great task, he was asked to rule over the people and reign as the Son of Heaven. It has been said that Yu was the founder of China's first **hereditary** dynasty known as the Xia (2000–1600 B.C.).

for their crops. The amphorae were then hung by leather straps from beams in the houses at Banpo. Using the postholes left in the fine loess soil by house construction, Chinese archaeologists have been able to reconstruct the houses.

The Shang

The first written historical records of China come from the Shang dynasty (1500–1050 B.C.). These records were carved on either the shoulder bones of cattle or tortoise shells. Most records tell of the efforts of Shang kings to foretell the future. The kings sought guidance and blessings from their ancestors in the spirit world on warfare, weather, and the success of the harvests. Their records give us a picture of Shang life on the banks of the Yellow and its tributaries.

Anyang, a Shang capital city, was located in the middle stretches of the Yellow River. This royal capital, the first site excavated by archaeologists in the People's Republic of China,

This oracle bone is made from a cow shoulder bone.

stands on a plain drained by three tributaries of the Yellow River. Archaeologists tested the soil and learned that the plain of Anyang had many plants at the time of the Shang. Also, the climate of the area was warmer and moister than it is today. Working with geologists, Chinese archaeologists have concluded that the course of the Yellow's tributaries changed over the centuries.

Shang records suggest that many of their settlements were located on a hill or a mound. The remains of more than one thousand water buffaloes, one hundred water deer, and many bamboo rats were found at Anyang. Because these animals all live in marshy areas, archaeologists concluded that the lowlands were wet and marshy with the waters of the Yellow and its tributaries.

More than three thousand years ago, the Shang people built large cities, developed major farming projects, and waged war. They grew millet—irrigated by the waters of the Yellow and its tributaries—and used the grain to make wine for drinking and ritual sacrifices. The Shang kings made sacrifices of grain, wine, and meat to their ancestors using decorated

This bronze bowl from the Shang dynasty was used for rituals.

bronze vessels. They also practiced human sacrifice. At Anyang, archaeologists analyzed the bones of these victims and concluded that many were young males, probably prisoners of war.

The Zhou

The Zhou lived in the middle stretches of the Yellow River and rose to power after the Shang. During the Zhou dynasty (1050–221 B.C.), seven states waged terrible wars. Zhou warfare was large in scale and brutal. Battles included chariots,

The Zhou dynasty made the middle stretches of the Yellow River their base.

crossbowmen, and calvary. Soldiers fought with swords, daggers, and axes. The halberd was the chief weapon of the Zhou. This was a blade mounted on a long pole. When a soldier swung this weapon at an enemy is caused great damage.

During this time, the great **sage** Confucius traveled from state to state with his philosophy, or set of ideas and beliefs about life. He hoped to persuade rulers to lead their people by being fair and just instead of by waging war. Confucius was born in the state of Lu, in today's Shandong Province where the waters of the Yellow River empty into the Bohai Sea.

Guide to War
The *Art of War*, the world's oldest military handbook, was written by Sun Zi, during the Zhou dynasty.

The first emperor of the Qin dynasty built his capital in the Wei River Basin, where the Yellow River and its major tributary—the Wei River—meet.

Chapter Three

Birth of an Empire

The long power struggle among the warring states of the Zhou dynasty, ended in 221 B.C. King Zheng of the state of Qin unified the states into a single government after defeating rival states. The king of Qin took the title of *Huangdi* (emperor). The ruler of every Chinese dynasty adopted this title until the twentieth century.

The dynasty was known as Qin (221–207 B.C.) from the feudal state the king ruled before conquering his neighboring states. The Qin capital, near today's Xian, was located in the Wei River Basin.

The Qin expanded the empire beyond its traditional home in the middle and lower stretches of the Yellow River. The first emperor began a series of reforms and building projects designed to unite China. He simplified the characters of various Chinese writing systems. And he unified a series of defensive walls to build the first sections of China's Great Wall.

The First Emperor's Tomb

The first emperor built himself a magnificent tomb near the banks of the Wei River. Farmers digging a well to tap into the water of the Wei River, the Yellow's major tributary, discovered this site by accident in 1974. Chinese archaeologists have found thousands of life-sized warriors made of pottery in pits surrounding the tomb. These figures, originally armed with real bronze weapons, are believed to have acted as guards for the spirit of the first emperor who died in 210 B.C. The tomb itself—with the emperor's body—remains untouched. Chinese archaeologists are waiting for technological advances that will allow them to build an arch to fully protect the huge site without damaging its structure.

Archaeologists have consulted records made by the historian Sima Qian from the Han dynasty (206 B.C.–A.D. 220). He describes the emperor's final resting place as a gigantic underground palace. According to the historian, the underground palace contains a **topographical map** of the Qin empire. In

This photo shows some of the sculptures that surround the first emperor's tomb.

Chinese Dragon

Western myth presents the dragon as a fire-breathing monster. But to the Chinese, the dragon is the divine Lord of the Waters. The Chinese dragon brings water to the parched earth after awakening from his winter sleep.

The first emperor's palace stood along the banks of the Wei River. Water was thus a lucky element for the Qin. The first emperor adopted the dragon as the imperial emblem. Throughout China's two thousand-year imperial history, all the emperors followed this practice.

this map, the Yellow and other rivers, made of mercury, flow into a miniature ocean. Above models of mountains and plains, there are pearls on the ceiling to represent the stars of the constellations.

The Han

The Han dynasty was China's first great dynasty, lasting more than four centuries. Today's Chinese still call themselves the Han people. The Han dynasty had two great capitals on the

An old bell tower sits among modern streets and buildings in Xian.

Yellow River. From 206 B.C. to A.D. 9, Chang'an—the ancient name for the city of Xian—was the capital and from A.D. 25 to 220, the capital city was Luoyang.

During the Han dynasty, the stability of the empire was based on engineering advances that controlled the waters of the China's rivers. These advances allowed Han emperors to begin a series of military conflicts and establish more settlements that expanded the borders of the empire. China's great rivers became the highways of the empire. A network of canals supplemented these water highways. Chinese boats of the Han

Farmers cut fields into the hillsides along the Yellow River, allowing more land to be cultivated.

dynasty used rudders, a steering device not seen in the West for another one thousand years.

Chinese of the Han dynasty sought ways to harness the water of rivers for irrigation. The **endless chain**, or turnover wheel, came into use about A.D. 100. To raise water from wells or ditches, two people turn a pedal that pulls a chain of square

wooden boards. The endless chain of wooden boards then pulls a stream of water uphill.

Farmers cut terraces into the hillsides to create more farmland. The long and narrow fields that wound around hillsides were watered by a series of the new irrigation devices. This irrigation helped expand the Han empire. Taxes were paid to the emperor in grain. The extra crops were shipped to supply the large Han armies.

Centered on the middle stretches of the Yellow River, the Han expanded Chinese territory. The empire extended to central Asia in the west, Mongolia in the north, Korea in the east, and Vietnam in the south.

Cradle of China

The middle stretches of the Yellow River are also known as the "cradle of China."

The Great Buddha in the Binglingsi caves is one of the many religious sites that can be found along the banks of the Yellow River.

Chapter Four

Sacred Sites

When the Han empire collapsed in A.D. 220, China became a divided country. During this time, the Yellow River became a crucial waterway for the empire in the north while the empire in the south relied on the Yangzi River. Many important northern Chinese families fled from their homes along the Yellow River to escape warfare and settled in the south along the Yangzi. During this period of political difficulties, many Chinese sought comfort and hope from religion. Many sites on the banks of the Yellow River reflect China's three major philosophies from this historical period

> **Five Sacred Mountains**
>
> The five great sacred mountains are located in central China. Each mountain corresponds to one of the five points on the Chinese compass: north, south, east, west, and center. Hua Shan (Mount Lotus) is in the west in Shaanxi Province, Heng Shan (Mount Heng) is in the south in Hunan Province, and Heng Shan (which sounds the same as Mount Heng in the south, but has a different Chinese character) is in the north in Shanxi Province. Song Shan (Mount Song), in the center of Henan Province, is the only one of the mountains not located along the Yellow River. Not far from the mouth of the Yellow River in Shandong Province lies Tai Shan (Mount Tai), most revered of the five sacred mountains of China. The ancient Chinese believed that the sun began its westward journey from a mountain beyond the East Sea. The emperor made offerings to heaven and earth on the summit of the mountain.

—Buddhism, Daoism, and Confucianism. Other sites along the Yellow, such as the five great sacred mountains, were the focus of cults that began in ancient times.

Buddhism

Buddhism is a religion based on the teachings of the *Buddha*—a name that means "the wise one" or "the enlightened one." It reached China from Nepal by way of the **Silk Roads**—a series of trade routes between China and central Asia. Foreign missionaries, merchants, and Chinese Buddhist pilgrims traveled along the Silk Roads. They brought holy books, foreign ideas, and new arts into China.

International trade thrived as products and ideas were carried by camel caravan across the dry, barren lands of the north

Silk Roads

Since no river provides safe travel across northern China, traders established the Silk Roads. The 4,000-mile (6,436-km) series of trade routes begin in Xian and connect north China with India and the eastern Mediterranean. Part of the roads still exist as a paved highway linking Pakistan and China.

Many people visit the caves at Lungmen each year.

by the Silk Roads. China exported silk, tea, porcelain, and lacquerware and imported precious metals, glass, and foreign ideas, including Buddhism. As the Chinese became influenced by Buddhist ideas, they began a series of vast building projects dedicated to Buddha.

One of the world's most impressive Buddhist sites lies 9 miles (14 km) south of Luoyang, on the Yi River, a tributary of the Yellow. At Lungmen, the rocky cliffs rise steeply from the banks of the Yi. More than 1,000 caves and 100,000 Buddhist images are carved into the cliffs. Construction of this site began at the end of the fifth century and lasted for three hundred years. Huge images of the Buddha look out over the river. Cliffs are honeycombed with religious carvings.

In Chang'an, the capital of the Tang dynasty (618-906) in the Wei River Basin, Buddhist towers called **pagodas** began to appear. The most well-known, the Big Goose Pagoda, was built in 652 to house religious texts brought to China by Xuan Zang, a Buddhist pilgrim. Xuan Zang traveled along the Silk Roads from 629 to 645 and brought back *sutras* (sacred Buddhist texts) from India. The Big Goose Pagoda was built to house these religious texts. At the Big Goose Pagoda, Buddhists translated the sacred texts from Sanskrit into Chinese, helping to spread the new religion.

The Big Goose Pagoda is located in Xian.

Chan Buddhism

Located south of the Yellow River, Shaolin Temple is the birthplace of Chan, or Zen, Buddhism. Chan Buddhism is heavily influenced by native Chinese philosophies, particularly Daoism. *Chan* comes from the Sanskrit word *dhyana*, meaning "meditation."

The Shaolin Temple houses the largest collection of **stupas** in China. Stupas are mounds in which the sacred remains of the Buddha or his disciples are enshrined. Shaolin Temple is said to have been founded by an Indian monk in the fifth century. To strengthen self-discipline and learn skills for self-defense, the monks at Shaolin Temple became masters of **gongfu** (kungfu). The term, as used today, includes martial arts and weapon wielding as well as various methods of staying healthy.

The origin of all gongfu styles can be traced back to the Shaolin Temple. There are internal and external styles of gongfu. Internal gongfu trains the mind and spirit, while external gongfu is said to exercise the tendons, bones, and skin.

Weather, neglect, and intentional destruction have damaged most of the Buddhist structures along the Yellow River. Throughout China's history, various groups have struggled for

A group of monks practice gongfu at the Shaolin Temple.

> **Gongfu**
>
> Many forms of external gongfu are inspired by the movements of animals found along the banks of the Yellow River. The tiger, panther, monkey, snake, and crane are all different styles of external gongfu.

control of the river because of its strategic location. Some ruling forces saw Buddhism as a threat to their power over the country, and sometimes took action against the practice of this religion. In A.D. 845 during the Tang dynasty, an anti-Buddhist movement destroyed 4,600 monasteries and 40,000 shrines, including many on the Yellow River and its tributaries.

In the early 1900s, foreign adventurers looted many Buddhist sculptures and stone carvings. Some of these are now in museums, art galleries, and private collections in the United States, Europe, and Japan. When the country became the People's Republic of China in 1949, some Buddhist artworks were sold to foreign collectors by the new Communist government. The Communist officials were only too pleased to rid China of religious relics in exchange for money to rebuild the country. The Communist government allowed further damage of Buddhist structures during the Cultural Revolution. From 1966 to 1976, the Red Guard—young people from China's cities on orders from the government—traveled throughout the country searching out and destroying temples, relics, and scriptures.

Daoism

According to Chinese tradition, *Laozi* (Old Master) lived around the same time as Confucius and founded the philosophy of Daoism. Daoists believe that people should follow the basic principles of the universe in order to live in harmony.

The Daoist Zhongyue Temple on the banks of the Yellow River is one of the oldest Taoist temples in China. Doubtless, Daoists chose this location because of its connection to Daoist principles—the *Dao*, which means "way," is often associated with water. The Daoist text *Daodejing, the Classic of the Way and Virtue* states:"There is nothing softer and weaker than water. And yet, overcoming that which is strong, nothing is superior to water."

Confucianism

Confucianism is a philosophy that focuses on righteousness and decency in human relationships. Having empathy for the sufferings of others and the courage to do what is right are the central concerns of Confucianism. This philosophy also encourages individuals to be responsible for their own actions and to honor their family obligations.

Confucianism played a part in every young man's education in imperial China. One of the four great Confucian institutions of learning, the Songyang Academy, is located south of the Yellow River. Here, young men studied Confucian classics and prepared for the imperial examinations for jobs in the government.

A Daoist priest visits Heng Shan, one of the five sacred mountains of China.

The Yellow River has inspired many Chinese writers and artists.

Chapter Five

In Art and Words

Throughout China's history, the waters and banks of the Yellow River have been subjects of art and literature. Poets and novelists have described the qualities of its rushing waters and the tranquility of its flowing tributaries. Painters have captured the waters and the rugged peaks that line its banks. Plants and animals nourished by the waters of the Yellow River play a large part in the arts of China. Some of these are unique to the Yellow River.

The Lac Tree

The lac, or varnish, tree thrives in the middle stretches of the Yellow. The sap of the lac tree has a beautiful gloss and a strong adhesive quality. It is called **lacquer**.

Lacquerware is produced by brushing layers of lacquer onto an object, often carved of wood. As the layers of lacquer build up, the object takes on a smooth and brilliant finish. The lacquerware is often carved, gilded, or painted.

An artist makes a lacquer panel.

Lacquerware

China's emperors valued lacquerware and liked to have it in their households. They even set up special workshops along the Yellow River to create lacquerware from the trees growing along its banks.

Chinese discovered early that lacquer could be used to protect objects and make them more beautiful. As far back as the Stone Age, the Chinese used lacquer to coat eating utensils, ornaments, and ritual objects. People used lacquer to coat writing implements, musical instruments, eating and drinking utensils, weaponry, furniture, and even transportation vehicles.

Landscape Painting

Much of Chinese art depicts the beauty of nature and the workings of the universe. The Chinese believe the world is composed of two forces—yin and yang—and that every being and object in the universe contains a balance of these two opposing, yet complementary forces. Yang is described as the male, active, hot force. Rocks and mountains are examples of yang. Yin is the female, passive, cool force, such as water. Chinese artists illustrate these forces in their paintings by including images of water alongside mountains and rocks.

For the Chinese, landscape painting is more than a picture of scenery. The paintings make a statement about the world, showing a place where all elements are in balance. Where mists rise from water meeting rock, the Chinese see the workings of the universe.

Shanshui

The Chinese term for landscape painting is *shanshui*, which means "mountains and water."

Water and mountains play an important role in many Chinese paintings.

Landscape paintings of the Northern Song dynasty (960–1276) often feature the Yellow River and the towering, majestic mountains of northern China. These landscapes depict the land carved by the waters of the Yellow River in northern China. Clear air, dry plains, and towering mountains characterize much of the northern Chinese landscape around the Yellow.

Gardens

The Chinese garden is designed to resemble a tiny universe within four walls. Just as a Chinese landscape painting depicts both mountains and rivers, a garden must contain both rocks and water. Traditional Chinese gardens also include plants, such as bamboo, plum blossom, and pine. The lure of a simple and solitary life in harmony with nature is the idea behind the building of walled-garden complexes.

The Tang dynasty scholar Lu Hong was much admired for his integrity and knowledge. Although the Tang emperor Xuan Zong asked Lu to serve in his government, he refused. Lu chose to live alone on Mount Song, outside the capital city of Luoyang on the southern bank of the Yellow River.

The emperor honored Lu by presenting him with a recluse's robe and a thatched hut built for him on Mount Song. Since that time, a walled garden in the town has become a favorite refuge for men of means who wish to escape the burdens of city life.

The Yellow in Literature

Li Dao-yuan, who died in 527, recorded the geography of all the major areas of China. Li wrote *The Guide to Waterways with Commentary*—a book that describes 1,389 rivers in China. His work is considered one of the major literary achievements of the Northern and Southern Dynasties period—from A.D. 220 to 581. He used official histories, philosophical statements, and biographies as well as supernatural tales, legends, and folk songs to tell about the Yellow River and other waterways.

One of Li's entries describes Dragon Gate on the Yellow River. Dragon Gate is said to have been opened up as a passage by Yu, the legendary founder of the Xia dynasty who tamed the waters of the Yellow River so long ago. According to legend, carp that swim upstream beyond this point turn into dragons. Using the dragon's role as an imperial symbol, the phrase "passing through Dragon Gate" came to mean success in a government career.

Poet Li Bai (701-762) of the Tang dynasty is one of the most beloved poets in Chinese history. He was known as "the Banished Immortal" for his extraordinary talent and poetic gifts. Traditional Chinese literary criticism compares his poems to the flow of a river. Critics cite its rushing energy, its tumbling fall, and its majestic flow. In the poem "Send in the Wine!" Li Bai evokes the qualities of the Yellow River, or the Huang he, to urge people to seize the joys of life:

Send in the Wine!
Have you never seen the waters of the Huang he, cascading from on high,
Rushing down to the sea, never to return.
Have you never seen in high towered bright mirrors, the lament of white hair,
In the morning like black silk, in the evening changed to snow.
In a man's life, to get the meaning, one must seize every joy,
Do not cause the golden wine-jar to sit empty in the moonlight.
Heaven has given me talents, they must be put to use,
A thousand gold exhausted, will return to me again.

(Translation by Richard A. Pegg)

Li Bai's poem written in Chinese, is read right to left, and in rows that run up and down.

The Grand Canal is still one of China's important waterways.

Chapter Six

Canals of the Yellow

Over the centuries, the Chinese built a series of canals to link the Yellow River system in the north to the Yangzi River system in the south. The main link of this waterway network is the Grand Canal. The Grand Canal is the oldest and longest artificial waterway in the world. Its construction lasted 1,779 years, from 486 B.C. to A.D. 1293. It is 1,115 miles (1,794 km) long. The Grand Canal and the Great Wall are magnificent engineering and organizational achievements of China.

Workers on the Canal

The Grand Canal, like the Great Wall, was built using forced labor. Even women had to help in its construction.

Today, people still use the canal to transport goods and for travel.

The Grand Canal connects China's capital city of Beijing in the north with the city of Hangzhou in the south. It links many rivers and tributaries into a network of waterways. These waterways include the Haihe, the Yellow, the Huai, the Yangzi and the Qiantang rivers. The Grand Canal, a fantastic feat of **hydroengineering**, actually reverses the flow of rivers from north to south.

The Grand Canal was built to carry rice and military troops from south China. In times of famine in north China, the Grand Canal was a lifeline. At the height of its activities during the Northern Song dynasty (960–1276), 330,000 tons of rice were shipped by the Grand Canal to the capital at Kaifeng on the Yellow River.

The Grand Canal also brought the benefits of irrigation. It promoted the development of economic and cultural cooperation between north and south China. Over the last century, however, stretches of the Grand Canal have silted up and become unusable.

China's Water Troubles

Today, China continues to struggle with water resources as well as with the flooding of the Yellow River. China has only 2,400 cubic meters of water per person—one-fourth of the world's average—because of the great difference between the water resources of the north and the south. Water is plentiful in south China, but scarce in north China. Water shortages in north China, especially in the Yellow River drainage area, can be crippling. In north China, the combined flow of the Yellow, Huai, and Haihe drainage areas is only 5.1 percent of the country's total water supply.

Modern economic development in China is based upon the exploitation of natural resources. Northern and northwestern China have the country's most abundant mineral and energy resources. These resources have yet to be fully exploited, however. The demand for water that

This tributary of the Yellow River has almost dried completely.

> **Breaking the Dams**
>
> In 1938, during the Japanese War of Aggression in China, Nationalist Army troops commanded by Chiang Kai-shek blew up the dikes of the Yellow River. Their goal was to halt the Japanese advance at any cost, but it resulted in the drowning of perhaps one million Chinese people. The dike was repaired with help from the United States in 1947. Today, the place where the dikes were broken has a floodgate to control the river waters. Etched into the embankment is an instruction from Mao Zedong, the Chinese Communist leader, "Control the Yellow River."

accompanies their development has hindered progress in the area. China's lack of adequate water resources in the north has also led to social and environmental problems. The Yangzi River Basin, which has water to spare, would be the ideal source for bringing water to the north.

Grand Water Projects

In 1996, the National People's Congress announced a hydroengineering project designed to divert water from south to north. Called the Grand Water Project, it is scheduled to be completed by the year 2010. The plan calls for three very large water diversion lines and each requires huge investments of labor and materials.

China has already committed itself to another major hydroengineering project. The Three Gorges Hydroelectric Dam Project on the Yangzi River is scheduled for completion in 2009. The project will displace nearly two million people from more than one thousand towns and villages along the Yangzi.

Together these hydroengineering projects promise to yield great future benefits for China. The projects will enhance economic development, improve environmental protection, foster social improvement, and control flooding. Hopefully, Chinese children of the twenty-first century will be able to enjoy the benefits of the waters of the Yellow River without having to fear its devastating floods. The term "China's Sorrow" will be just a name in their history books.

Workers build the Three Gorges Hydroelectric Dam on the Yangzi River.

Timeline

4800–2500 B.C.	Early Chinese people live in Banpo Village.
circa 2000–1600 B.C.	Yu controls the waters and starts the Xia Dynasty.
1500–1050 B.C.	The Shang dynasty rules China.
circa 1400–1050 B.C.	Anyang is the capital of the Shang dynasty.
circa 1050–221 B.C.	The Zhou dynasty rules China.
486 B.C.	Construction begins on the Grand Canal.
221–206 B.C.	The Qin dynasty rules a unified China.
206 B.C.–A.D. 220	Han Dynasty rules China; adopts Confucianism as state philosophy.
220-581	Buddhism spreads along the Yellow River during the era of Northern and Southern dynasties.
618–907	The Tang dynasty rules China.
960–1276	The Northern Song dynasty rules part of China.
1127–1279	The Southern Song dynasty rules part of China.
1921	The Communist Party is founded.
1938	Chiang Kai-shek breaks the dikes of the Yellow River.
1949	Mao Zedong proclaims the People's Republic of China.
1990s	China begins the Grand Water Project and Three Gorges Hydroengineering Project

Glossary

amphora—a two-handled jug used to store liquids

Anyang—the last capital city of the Shang, located by the Yellow River

Banpo—a large Stone Age site located in the Wei River Basin

culture heroes—legendary figures who were said to have discovered fire and invented farming, hunting, and fishing

dhyana—the Buddhist practice of meditation

dike—an embankment to protect low land from flooding

endless chain—a turnover wheel that raises water for irrigation, which came into use about A.D. 100

gongfu—martial arts that includes boxing, weapon wielding, and ways to stay healthy

hereditary—something passed on from parent to child

hydroengineering—the design, construction, and manipulation of running water

lacquer—the sap of the lac tree, which is painted onto a wooden object to produce lacquerware

loess—a yellow, sandy silt

mouth—the point where a river empties into the sea

pagoda—a type of tower-shaped Buddhist structure

sage—a wise person

Silk Roads—a series of trade routes that connected north China with India and the eastern Mediterranean

source—the point where a river originates

stupa—a mound that enshrines the sacred remains of the Buddha or one of his disciples

sutra—a sacred text of Buddhism

topographical map—a type of map that shows the natural land and water forms of a place

tributary—a stream or river flowing into a larger stream or river

To Find Out More

Books

Blunden, Caroline and Mark Elvin. *Cultural Atlas of China*. Oxford: Phaidon Press, 1983.

Clunas, Craig. *Art in China*. Oxford, New York: Oxford University Press, 1997.

Cotterell, Arthur. *Ancient China*. New York: Alfred A. Knopf, 1994.

Debaine-Francfort, Corinne. *The Search for Ancient China*. New York: Harry N. Abrams, Inc., Publishers, 1999.

Dramer, Kim. *People's Republic of China*. Danbury, CT: Children's Press, 1999.

Hook, Brian, ed. *The Cambridge Encyclopedia of China*. Cambridge: Cambridge University Press, 1991.

Smith, Christopher J. *China: People and Place in the Land of One Billion*. Boulder: Westview Press, 1991.

Strassberg, Richard E., translator. *Inscribed Landscapes: Travel Writing from Imperial China*. Berkeley: University of California Press, 1994.

Zhao, Songqiao. *Geography of China: Environment, Resources, Population, and Development*. New York: John Wiley & Sons, 1994.

Videotapes/CD-ROMs

The Power of Place. The Annenberg/CPB Collection. P.O. Box 2345, S. Burlington, VT 05407-2345. Twenty-six part-series of videos examining World Regional Geography from a case study perspective.

Yellow Earth. A film about the hardships of life along the Yellow River on the loess plateau. Beijing: China Film Export & Import Corp., 1985; Palo Alto, CA: China Video Movies Distributing Co.

Organizations and Online Sites

Asia Society

http://www.asiasociety.org

This organization offers art exhibitions, films, programs for teachers and students, and information on Asia.

Ask Asia

http://www.askasia.org

This online site for children in kindergarten through high school provides a wealth of resources and cultural information on Asia, including games, activities, and links to relevant people, places, and institutions.

International Rivers Network
1847 Berkeley Way
Berkeley, CA 94703

http://www.irn.org

This organization's mission is to protect river systems and to increase understanding, awareness, and respect for rivers.

National Geographic

http://www.nationalgeographic.com/maps/index.html

From the online site for the *National Geographic* magazine, you can explore maps and information on countries around the world, including China.

Silkroad Foundation
P. O. Box 2275
Saratoga, CA 95070
http://www.silk-road.com
On this organization's online site, you can view maps of the famous trade routes, the Silk Roads, and a timeline of the region.

A Note on Sources

As a doctoral candidate at Columbia University, I have access to some of the world's finest library collections on China, including the C.V. Starr East Asian Library. Yet I find it is always best to start out research with a very general book or even an encyclopedia entry. The main points of interest in such a book or article can be turned into ideas for chapter organization. Then I consult more specialized books for each chapter.

The history of mankind is the history of people and water. Like our earliest ancestors, we are dependent upon water for food and transportation. The development of China's infrastructure in the modern age depends upon water as a main resource.

Spectacular archaeological finds along the course of the Yellow River link the past and present with the river's waters. As an art historian, I wanted to use artifacts to show readers how China's past and present are linked with the course of the Yellow River. I was able to use Chinese archaeological reports on sites such as Banpo, Anyang, and Li Shan.

—Kim Dramer

Index

Numbers in *italics* indicate illustrations.

agriculture, 10–11, *10*, 15, *28–29*, 29
amphorae, 16–17
animal life, 18–19, 39
Anyang (Shang capital city), 17
archaeology, 15–20
art, 39, 41–43
artifacts, *16*, *18*, *19*, 20, *25*

Bai, Li, 44
Banpo community, 16, *16*
Big Goose Pagoda, 34, *34*
Bohai Sea, 8, 21
bridges, 15
Buddhism, *30*, 32–34. See also Chan Buddhism.

calligraphy, 8, *8*, 45
canals, 27, *46*, 47

Chan Buddhism, 34–36. See also Buddhism.
Chang'an (Tang capital city), 34. See also Xian.
Confucianism, 37
Confucius, 21
Cultural Revolution, 36
culture heroes, 17

Daodejing, the Classic of the Way and Virtue (Laozi), 36
Daoism, 36–37, *37*
dikes, 8–9, *9*, 50
dragon, 26, *26*
Dragon Gate, 44

endless chain, 28

flooding, 8, 15

61

gardens, 43
Gobi Desert, 7
gongfu, 35–36, *35*
Grand Canal, *46*, 47–49, *48*
Grand Water Project, 50
Great Buddha, *30*
Great Wall, 24, 47
Guide to Waterways with Commentary, The (Li Tao-yuan), 44

Han dynasty, 24, 26–29, 31
Heng Shan (holy place), 32, *37*
Hong, Lu, 43
Hua Shan (Mount Lotus), 32
Huang he. *See* Yellow River.
hydroengineering, 48, 50

irrigation, 10–11, *10*, 19, 28, 49

Kaifeng (Song capital city), *9*, 48
Kaishek, Chiang, 50
kungfu. *See* gongfu.

lac tree, 40

lacquer, 40
lacquerware, 40–41, *40*
Laozi (Old Master), 36
literature, 39, 44–45
loess soil, 7, 17
Lungmen, 33, *33*
Luoyang (Han capital city), 27, 43

millet, 10, 19

natural resources, 49
Northern Dynasty, 44
Northern Song Dynasty, 43, 48

oracle bones, *18*

pagodas, 34, *34*
plant life, 39

Qian, Sima, 24
Qin dynasty, 23–24
Qinghai Lake, 14
Qinghai Province, 7

rafts, 14, *14*
Red Guard, 36
religion. *See* Buddhism; Confucianism; Daoism.

Send in the Wine! (Li Bai), 45
Shandong Province, 21
Shang dynasty, 17–20, *19*
shanshui (landscape painting), 42
Shaolin Temple, 34–35, *35*
Silk Roads, 32–33
silt, 8, 49, *49*
Song Shan (Mount Song), 32
Songyang Academy, 37
Southern Dynasty, 44
Stone Age, 15
stupas (burial mounds), 34
sutras (scared texts), 34

Tai Shan (Mount Tai), 32
Tang dynasty, 36, 43–44
Tao-yuan, Li, 44
Three Gorges Hydroelectric Dam Project, 50–51, *51*
Tibetan Plateau, 7–8, *12*, 13
topographical map (of Qin empire), 24, 26
turnover wheel. *See* endless chain.

Wei River Basin, 15, *22*, 34

Xia dynasty, 17
Xian (Han capital city), 27, *27*, 34. *See also* Chang'an.
Xingsuhai region, 13

Yangzi River, 31, 47, 50
Yangzi River Basin, 50
Yellow River, *9*, *10–11*, *20–21*, *28–29*, *38*, *42*
  length of, 11
  mouth of, 8
  source of, 7
  tributaries of, 15, 18
Yi River, 33
yin and yang, 41
Yu (culture hero), 17

Zang, Xuan, 34
Zedong, Mao, 50
Zen Buddhism. *See* Chan Buddhism.
Zhongyue Temple, 37
Zhou dynasty, 20–21, *20–21*, 23
Zong, Xuan, 43

About the Author

Kim Dramer lives on the banks of the Hudson River in New York City. Here, she is a Ph.D. candidate at Columbia University in the Department of Art History and Archaeology. She is writing her doctoral dissertation on ancient Chinese art and architecture. While researching her thesis, she has traveled in China, visiting many sites along the Yellow River. She is pictured here in front of the Big Goose Pagoda mentioned on page 34.

As the mother of twins, Wang Xianhan and Wang Xiantang, she is particularly interested in helping young people learn about China. She has written many books on China, including *Games People Play: China* and *Enchantment of the World: China* for Children's Press. She is also the author of *The Mekong River* for the Watts Library series.